The Goldflower Adventures:

THE RAINBOW AMULET

by Chiffon Strickland Jenkins
illustrated by MikeMotz.com

Volume 2

This book is dedicated to the
Strickland and Jenkins families and friends.
"Our hearts are touched,
we thank you much because
without you, there is no us,"
Love, The Goldflower Adventure Kids.

THE RAINBOW AMULET

by Chiffon Strickland Jenkins

illustrated by MikeMotz.com

Table of Contents

THE RAINBOW AMULET

1

The Flashing Light

Olivia's alarm clock was ringing loudly. It was already 6:30 am, and she didn't want to get up for school. As she reached over to turn off the alarm, she paused for a brief moment as she vaguely remembered the sounds of a whistle and screams. She thought to herself, *It must have been from a dream.*

Olivia loved learning, but she dreaded going to school. In fact, she thought it was one of the most boring things on Earth. If she could have life her way, it would involve going on endless adventures in far-away, unexplored lands, with creatures and danger lurking at every corner.

As she slowly pulled back the blanket and fumbled to place her feet in her slippers, she could hear her mom yelling from downstairs. Every morning at 6:35 am, without fail, her mom would say, "Olivia Kennedy, you better get up and get dressed. We don't have all day, Little Lady."

And without fail, Olivia would reply, "Yes, Ma'am. I'll be ready in five minutes tops." This was her morning ritual, Monday through

Friday. Getting dressed was a chore in deciding what to wear: pants, shorts, a skirt, or a dress?

She was a free spirit—easygoing—but not very fashionable. Comfort was more important than matching her socks with her blouse. It was days like this when she wished she could get fashion tips from her friend, Ming -Lin. If there were an award for best-dressed third-grader, it would undoubtedly go to Ming-Lin. Her mom was a designer, so fashion came easy to her—it was in her blood. She would wear a red dress with cute shoes, and of course, matching hairpins and ribbons. Ribbons and hairpins were her signature fashion piece; she made them herself.

Since Ming-Lin wasn't there to help, Olivia decided to put on the clothes that her mom had ironed the night before. After her mom called out to her for the third time, she knew it was time to get her behind downstairs. Her mom was a literature professor and often spoke at conferences, so being on time for everything was important to her.

"Were you daydreaming again, Little Lady?" her mom asked. "We are five minutes late already. Grab your backpack and let's go."

She reached into her backpack to make sure she had the goldflower watch that she found a few months ago at her grandmother's house. She couldn't go anywhere without it—it made her feel safe, but she wasn't quite sure why. Finding it at her Gran's house made it special enough.

While looking out the car window on the way to school, Olivia saw a light flicker in one of the treetops. Her curiosity wouldn't let her turn away. The light was there, then gone again. Olivia's mind was racing. *Could it be a distress signal?* She continued to look back over her shoulder until the tree was out of sight. The mystery and intrigue was exciting to Olivia. Maybe her mind was playing tricks on her, but maybe not. She and her Dad would watch old classic movies, and things like this would happen in those.

She couldn't wait to get to school now so she could tell her best friend, Josie, what she had seen.

As she arrived, Josie was standing at the door waiting for her. Josie and Olivia had been friends since preschool. They liked all of the same things—well, almost all. You see, Josie loved playing baseball. Anything that had to do with baseball made her happy. Her dad was the coach for her team, and Josie was the star pitcher and captain.

"Guess what I saw," whispered Olivia. Before Josie could reply, Olivia blurted out, "A distress signal."

"A what?" replied Josie.

Olivia explained how she saw the light flashing from the top of the tree. Josie placed her hand on Olivia's shoulder.

"Now, we've been friends forever, and I know that you have quite an imagination, but this is just a little too much for a Monday morning. It was probably just the sunlight bouncing off of something stuck in the tree."

Becoming agitated with Josie's reply, Olivia walked away shaking her head.

"Wait up! I'm not trying to be mean, but I'm just saying."

"Don't worry about it. Just forget that I

even mentioned it. I'll share my news with the others. Marvin and Alex will understand. They watch lots of detective and superhero movies, and they know all about secret codes and spy techniques from their comics."

Now Josie was getting upset. She half-heartedly replied, "You're being silly. It's not that I don't believe you. It's just strange that something like that would happen around here."

"Amazing things can happen anywhere at any time. Just last week, we read our first chapter book about a little boy who was lost in the ocean for days. No one thought he would ever be found, but he was eventually saved. Sure, he was scared and had almost given up, but he believed that rescuers would come for him and that he would see his family again. Maybe the distress signal was someone reaching out to me—to us—for help."

Josie apologized, "You're right, I can be a little harsh at times. I guess I'm just not in a good mood after my little sister ruined my leaf project. I can't believe she flushed all of my leaves down the toilet. My parents said I shouldn't get upset with her, since she's only two and didn't know what she was doing was wrong. Little sisters can be a pain at times. I love her, but gosh, she's always getting into my stuff. I had to put a lock on my baseball card box last week when she was looking at them with peanut butter and jelly all over her hands. I know you are glad that you are an only child."

"I'm sorry; I had forgotten about that. I'll tell you what, let's meet after school today, and I'll help you get more leaves. We'll invite Ming-Lin to go with us, and it'll be fun." They gave each other a big hug and a high-five.

As they walked into the classroom, they saw Isabella, Maria, and Ming-Lin waving. Ming -Lin was putting a ribbon that she had made in Maria's hair. She glued her ribbons to fancy hairpins; they were so pretty, and all of the girls liked them. If she played her cards right, she could be a fashion mogul by the fifth grade and would be worth hundreds of dollars. She'd be rich enough to buy that new bike she wanted— the one with the flowery basket and glittery tassels coming out of the handlebars. But she'd have to start selling the hair accessories instead of giving them away. She always said she enjoyed making them for fun, not for money.

"Good morning, class. Please take your seats, since the bell has rung," said Ms. Ellis. She was one of their favorite teachers. She had a way of making the lessons easier to understand—even those dreaded fractions! As Ms. Ellis started calling morning attendance, Olivia sat sluggishly in her desk with her chin propped up in her hand, aimlessly staring out the window. She could hear Ms. Ellis going down the list: *Amy Adams, here, Lisa Berry, here, Casey Cross, here, David Evans, here,* but her voice was slowly disappearing and sounded like it was way off in the distance. Olivia thought to herself, *I wish school lessons were more than numbers, words, and maps. Why couldn't it be more of an adventure—yes, an adventure!*

2

The Thunder

Olivia could hear thunder, and lightning, from time to time, streaked across the sky. Suddenly, she heard someone calling her name: "Olivia... Olivia." She continued walking toward the sound of the voice. She soon discovered that it was Josie and Ming-Lin, and they were in a tree!

"Why are you guys up there?" asked Olivia as she shook her head in amusement.

"It's because of the…" Josie fearfully replied as she struggled to complete her sentence.

In a very nervous voice, Olivia asked, "The what?"

"Don't you see it? It's over there, behind that rock," murmured Josie.

Olivia looked but didn't see anything. She commanded, "Come down, there's nothing." But before she could finish her thought, a loud noise—almost like a roar—came out of nowhere. They all screamed uncontrollably as Olivia scampered up the tree with them.

"I'm scared," said Ming-Lin nervously. They sat silent for a few minutes, and then Olivia looked into her backpack and pulled out her watch.

Ming-Lin asked, "What are you doing?"

"I'm calling for help," replied Olivia.

Josie looked at her, puzzled, and asked in a doubtful voice, "With a watch?"

"Trust me, it will work," Olivia assured her.

Olivia held it in her hand while looking up at the sky. The goldflower on the watch started to glow. With a big smile on her face, Olivia said, "We're going to be okay now."

They remained in the tree for a few more minutes, just to make sure that the coast was clear. As they looked around surveying the area, they decided that it was safe to make their way home. They carefully climbed down the tree one at a time.

When they reached the ground, Ming-Lin asked, "How did you make the watch glow?"

Olivia smiled, gave her a quick wink, and said, "Let's go before it gets too dark!"

The thunder and lightning had stopped. There was a silence—one might even say a sense of stillness—in the air. After walking for a while, once again, they found themselves back at the same tree.

Josie said, "I think we're lost."

Ming-Lin tearfully replied, "I'm scared and hungry. My new shoes are dirty. I have leaves and bugs in my hair. I want to go home and get in my soft, warm, cozy bed."

Doing her best to comfort Ming-Lin, Olivia reached for her hand. "It will be okay. We will get out of here soon. I promise!"

"Maybe your fancy, shimmering watch can get us out of this mess," said Josie.

"One thing's for sure: Being negative

won't help us," Olivia replied.

With her head held low, Josie apologized, "I'm sorry. It's just that I'm tired, and I'm going to miss my baseball game if we don't get out of here. You know I get frustrated when things don't work out as planned."

They seemed to have lost track of time. They could hear the owls calling out to each other. The crickets and other tiny creatures were also singing their evening songs. The sky was now clear, and the stars were out. They were very tired, hungry, cold, and sleepy. But just as they thought they couldn't go any farther, they saw a light shining in the distance. They reluctantly agreed to walk toward it, and together, brave the unknown.

3

The Tree House

To their surprise, the light was coming from a house—a house in a tree, to be exact. They approached the dwelling, holding hands tightly. They called out, "Hello, is anyone there?" They looked at each other, and then said it again, but louder this time. "Hello, is anyone there?"

"Stop! What do you want here?" The words rang out from an unfriendly voice inside of the tree house.

Olivia's big brown eyes widened as she exclaimed, "We are lost, and we just want to find our way home." A few seconds passed, and then a rope ladder was lowered and down came one figure after another.

First, a small boy appeared. "Hello, I am Marvin—Marvin the Marvelous!" he said proudly, with his chest out and head held high. He had big, almond-shaped eyes, a gentle smile, and dreadlocks. He kept one hand in his pocket as he introduced the others. "This is Alex and the twins, Isabella and Maria. What are you doing in our forest?"

"Your forest? We didn't know this was your forest," replied Josie with both hands firmly on her hips.

"We are trying to get home, but we can't find our way. Can you help us?" Olivia said in a very calm voice.

"How do we know that you're not spies?" asked Alex.

Josie replied, "Spies? Why would we be spies? That's nonsense."

"We have to protect our forest from the..." said the twins in unison.

Marvin winked and shook his head at the twins, motioning for them to be quiet. He didn't know why the girls were at their camp, but they seemed innocent enough and didn't appear dangerous at first glance. They hardly knew them, though, and it didn't make sense to tell them about the mysteries of the forest. Besides, they would be gone soon. He then nodded at Alex.

"Never mind; if you're not spies, then we can let you pass," said Alex.

"But we don't know how to get home! Can you tell us the way? We haven't had anything to eat, and we're tired," pleaded Ming-Lin.

"If it's not too much trouble, could we spend the night and get an early start in the morning?" asked Olivia.

Not sure of what to say, Marvin and Alex excused themselves. They walked over and sat under a tree to chat in private.

"First, they wanted directions, and now they want to stay the night," debated Alex.

"Yes, I know, but what should we do? It's dark, and something could happen to them," replied Marvin. "We would never forgive ourselves if we didn't help them."

"I guess you're right. We're always talking about being protectors; now is as good a time as any. They do seem harmless and genuinely lost," agreed Alex.

The guys returned to the group to relay the news. The twins smiled with excitement, "*Bienvenidos a nuestra casa!* Welcome to our house!"

They all climbed up the ladder and into the tree house.

"We have food. Please sit down and make yourselves at home," offered the twins.

As they were eating their sandwiches, Olivia asked, "How long have you been living here?"

Marvin replied, "We've been here for a long time. We have to protect the forest now."

Olivia asked curiously, "From what?"

Alex interrupted with a question, "What were you doing in the forest?"

Josie responded, "We were out looking for leaves for our school project, and we got lost. Ming-Lin and I heard a loud noise and climbed into a tree. Then Olivia came along, and once we thought that it was safe, we tried to find our way home."

The twins asked, "Where was the tree?"

"I don't know, but it was near a big rock," said Olivia.

Marvin, Alex, Isabella, and Maria all looked at each other.

"A big rock?" asked Marvin.

"Yes, a big rock. If you've seen one rock, you've seen another. They all look alike to me!" hissed Josie.

The room got very quiet. Then, innocently, Ming-Lin asked, "Aren't you afraid to live out here alone?"

"Afraid? No, we're not afraid. We can take care of ourselves. That's what protectors do," said Marvin. Alex looked at Marvin cautiously, hoping that he wouldn't share too much information with their new visitors.

"Protectors? What's all this babble about protectors?" asked Josie as she walked over to the window to separate herself from the others. She was starting to get irritable.

Trying not to wear out their welcome, Olivia said, "I'm sorry; we're asking too many questions. We don't mean to impose or seem nosey; we're just curious, that's all." Olivia looked over and noticed that Ming-Lin and the twins were yawning. "Well, it's getting late. We better get some sleep."

"Yes, I'm so tired I could sleep standing up," Ming-Lin replied.

"You don't have to do that," replied the twins. "We have extra sleeping bags, and you guys can use them."

"That's very kind of you. We really appreciate all that you guys have done for us. It's been a very stressful day," said Olivia.

They agreed that it was time to get some rest and made preparations for bed.

At first, it was hard for Olivia to close her eyes—so much was racing through her mind! The room was semi-dark; the glow from the moon gave a sliver of light. She took a deep breath as she looked around at her friends and then over at the others. She knew she had to be strong for them and not let fear get in the way.

She rubbed the glass on her goldflower watch as she slowly drifted off to sleep.

4

A New Day

There was the smell of eggs and smoke from a small fire in the air. It seemed as though they had just lain down, but the sun was already shining brightly through the small windows of the tree house. The birds were chirping, and you could hear water splashing and what sounded like someone gargling. Olivia tiptoed over to the window and saw Marvin cooking while the twins brushed their teeth and washed their faces. Alex was walking up the path with a bucket of water. Olivia gently shook Ming-Lin and Josie to wake them.

"Wow, something smells good!" exclaimed Josie excitedly.

"Yes, it smells very good. I'm so hungry!" said Ming-Lin. They rushed down the ladder.

"Hola," greeted the twins with their mouths still filled with toothpaste.

"Did you sleep well?" asked Marvin.

"My back hurts. That sleeping bag was not comfortable," Josie said truthfully as she stretched and yawned.

"It smells great. What are you cooking?"

asked Olivia.

"It's my specialty. I call them Marvin's Marvels."

Looking over into the pan, Josie said, "They look like eggs to me."

Rubbing their stomachs, Ming-Lin, Isabella, and Maria said in unison, "Let's eat!" They all washed their hands in the bucket of water and then sat down for breakfast.

"Thanks again for letting us spend the night. We really appreciate it and hope that it wasn't much of a bother," Olivia said.

"No bother at all," Marvin responded with a smile.

After breakfast, Josie and the twins washed the dishes while the others straightened up the tree house.

"I guess we should be going soon. We

need to get home," said Ming-Lin.

"Yes, we better get going," Olivia agreed.

"We will take you only to the end of the path. After that, you will have to go the rest of the way alone," heeded Alex. "It should lead you back to the rock where you were collecting leaves for your project, but stay on the path so that you won't get lost again and don't stop for anyone or anything. There are things in the forest—some are good, and some are bad. Everyone will not be as nice and helpful as we are, so you have to be careful. We try to protect, but others only want to do harm. But since you are leaving, there's no need for details. Just remember what I said." Alex's tone was very serious as he spoke to the girls.

They gathered their things and started off on the journey. Marvin and Alex were leading the group. As they walked along, the two of them surveyed the surroundings with sharp eyes. Ming-Lin and the twins were laughing and talking, picking up small rocks and leaves along the way.

"They are so strange," Josie whispered.

"Who?" asked Olivia.

"Marvin and Alex. I mean, look at them; they keep looking back at us. Something is up with them, but I just can't put my finger on it. Why did he give us that speech about being careful, but wouldn't tell us why?" questioned Josie.

"I think they're nice. You're on edge about missing your game. If it's not going your way, then it's not a good day for any of us. I know you're the captain of your baseball team, so you are used to being the leader, but this is not a game. Think about it: They didn't have to let us stay, and they were kind enough to show us the way back home. Doesn't that count for something?" replied Olivia.

"Yeah, but I still don't trust them," Josie countered. "Marvin thinks he's some kind of superhero, and Alex acts like a know-it-all. I'm going to keep an eye on them both."

"Stop!" commanded Marvin as he also motioned with his arm for them to halt.

"*Qué te pasa?* What's wrong?" murmured the twins.

Marvin gestured for everyone to be silent. The bushes started to move, and they could hear footsteps and small tree limbs breaking. They all froze, they held their breaths, and their eyes widened. They didn't move a single inch. Ming-Lin grabbed Olivia's hand, squeezing it tighter and tighter. Marvin looked around, as if he was looking for a place for them to run. You could hear their hearts beating fast, and as the noise got louder and closer, their hearts beat faster and faster. Then, out of nowhere, something came scurrying out of the brush. The girls screamed like they had never screamed before.

The twins yelled, "*Mirada, mirada.* Look, look."

It was a family of deer, racing through the forest. There were three of them: a mother deer and two fawns.

"Oh my, I thought we were goners!" exclaimed Josie as she wiped the nervous sweat from her forehead.

"Me, too," laughed Olivia.

"Not me. I wasn't afraid," Marvin replied as he held his hand firmly in his right pocket.

"If you weren't afraid, why are you sweating? You looked scared to me," teased Josie.

Embarrassed and annoyed, Marvin started walking. Seeing that Marvin was upset, Alex commandingly said, "Let's keep moving. We're wasting time."

5

Creek of Blossoms

They walked until they came upon a creek with beautiful flowers and clusters of small trees that lined the bank. "This place is called the Creek of Blossoms," explained Marvin. "A long time ago, a family of fairies lived here. They had the ability to grow flowers with gorgeous blossoms in any color that you could imagine. There was even a flower that had all of the colors of the rainbow. When it bloomed, the sky was clear, and not a cloud could be seen for miles.

"Then, something terrible happened," he continued. "The clouds came, the sky got dark, the thunder and lightning started, and it rained for a very long time. The clouds blocked the sun, and the Rainbow Flower started to die. The fairies didn't know what to do. There was magic in the flower that made everything beautiful and full of life. The fairies would harvest the magic pollen from the Rainbow Flower, but the heavy rain had knocked off all of the petals. Several more days passed without sunlight, and the darkness fell upon them. As the Rainbow Flower withered away, the fairies slowly disappeared. Sometimes, on a windy day, you can hear whispers—soft, gentle whispers—as the breeze blows," said Marvin, as he cupped his hand to his ear.

"I hear it now," said Josie, as she mocked Marvin's gestures.

"What is it saying?" asked Ming-Lin.

"It's saying, 'Let's go because I have another baseball game tonight,'" Josie replied sarcastically.

"Josie! That's not nice," said Olivia, as she shook a pointed finger at her.

"I know you guys don't believe that crazy story. He's just making it all up. I don't believe it," Josie said, as she reached for her backpack and started to walk away.

The twins yelled, "Wait! Wait for us!"

The others followed. They passed tree after tree — so many trees, in fact, that they all started to look alike. "Are we lost?" Josie asked Marvin and Alex.

"No, we're not lost," shouted Marvin, but in his mind, he wasn't so sure.

"My feet hurt," said Ming-Lin.

"*Nuestros pies también.* Ours, too," agreed the twins.

Alex looked at Marvin. "Maybe we should take a break."

Reluctantly, Marvin agreed, but he didn't sit with the group. Instead, he sat alone. He had something shiny in his hand that he was rubbing, and he was mumbling something to himself as he rubbed it.

Olivia walked up behind him. "Are you alright?"

Startled to hear her voice, he quickly put it back in his pocket. "Yes, I'm okay. I'm just thinking."

Olivia tried to reassure him. "It will be okay. I know you will get us out of here. We all get confused sometimes."

Marvin replied, "Confused? I'm not confused! We're almost there. That Josie is starting to get on my last nerve, though. How dare she assume that I don't know the way and that we're lost! We're not lost!"

She could tell that he wasn't only trying to convince her that he knew the way, but he was also trying to convince himself. She placed her hand on his shoulder. "Let's go back to the others. We should really get moving."

6

The Growlers

This time, Olivia was walking up front with Marvin and Alex. Josie was still a little mad, so she walked behind Ming-Lin and the twins.

Olivia asked, "So how did you meet Isabella and Maria?"

"We all grew up together," responded

Marvin. "We're all that's left of our families. We lived here in the forest with our parents and grandparents. Then, the day of darkness came. We were out playing when it happened. After what seemed like a few hours, we walked back home, but no one was there. Everyone was just . . . gone," Marvin solemnly explained.

"Did they leave a note?" asked Olivia.

"No, they were just gone. But our families are still with us. They are in our hearts and our minds. The memories that we have of them keep us strong," answered Alex as he twisted the end of his shirt.

As they approached a fork in the road, they became unsure of which way to go. Marvin reached in his right pocket. He glanced to the left, and then to the right. This area of the forest was unfamiliar to him. He had never been this far from the tree house, but he was ashamed to admit it to the others. He thought to himself, *I'm Marvin the Marvelous. I can do this.* He paused for a moment and then vigorously said, "We go left."

"Are you sure?" asked Josie.

"Yes, I'm sure," Marvin answered confidently.

"Okay, to the left it is," replied Alex.

They all followed Marvin and took the path to the left. "This road looks different. Where are all of the flowers?" asked Ming-Lin.

They couldn't hear any birds singing or see any butterflies or squirrels. In fact, the only animals that they saw were a spooky-looking crow and an owl perched in a tree. To make matters worse, it had started to rain, and they could hear thunder off in the distance.

"I don't like this place," Ming-Lin sighed as she grabbed for Olivia's hand.

Marvin motioned for them to stop again. "I hear something," he said.

"Oh, you do? It's probably the deer family again," Josie laughed.

Marvin tiptoed over to a huge rock and waved for the others to follow. As they hid behind the boulder, they could hear heavy breathing and footsteps. It sounded like hundreds and hundreds of them. Suddenly, several huge creatures appeared out of the brush. They stood about 10 feet tall with large horns. They were hairy—like a bear—with big, black eyes, long claws, and a nose similar to a pig. They breathed deeply, and they grunted even louder—in fact, the sound of heavy breathing and grunts rang out repetitively, almost as if it was a matching

chant. The ground was shaking as the creatures pounded each step into the dry earth.

The children could feel their hearts beating from fear—sweat running down the sides of their faces, the hair standing up on the backs of their necks, hands and legs trembling. The urge to run or scream was strong, but they didn't dare.

As the creatures passed closer and closer to their hiding spot, Ming-Lin and the twins couldn't hold it in any longer. The mere sight of the creatures being so close was too much for them. They started to cry uncontrollably.

"Please, you guys have to pull it together," pleaded Olivia.

"Shhhhhh," said Josie, as she placed her finger up to her lips. "What are we going to do?"

"I think I see a place for us to run. Are you guys ready? Time is not on our side right now," said Alex.

Marvin looked over and saw the opening to a small cave. They pointed toward it, so the others could see.

"On three," commanded Marvin.

They all nodded.

The creatures were after them before they had even taken five steps! They were huge but fast, and the force of their pounding steps only increased. Now, their heavy breathing and grunts sounded more like intense growls.

"Hurry, run faster," shouted Marvin.

"We're almost there. Run, run, don't look back!" echoed Alex.

Ming-Lin's hand slipped away from Olivia's. "Wait! Please slow down, I think my shoe is coming off," she yelled.

Olivia looked back briefly and slowed down enough to grab her hand again. "It will be okay, just wiggle your foot back into your shoe."

"I'm trying! I'm trying!"

Josie and the twins raced by them. "Come on, no time for chatter. Those THINGS are on our heels!"

No sooner had Josie finished shouting then there was a loud growl, and everything seemed to move in slow motion. Right as they reached the opening of the cave, the creatures grabbed all of them.

"Put us down you stupid beasts!" bellowed Josie.

"Help! Help!" shouted the twins.

Overwhelmed with fear, Ming-Lin couldn't say a word. The terrified look on her face filled Olivia's eyes with tears as she reached out for her over one of the creature's shoulder. Marvin and Alex were hitting the creatures with their fists as they carried the children back to their lair. Who knew what kind of trouble was waiting for them there?

7

The Cage

As they sat locked in a cage, they noticed a huge pot of red liquid boiling over an open fire. Ming-Lin and the twins were sobbing uncontrollably.

"You guys have to calm down," said Olivia. Although she was terrified as well, she thought back to that day when her gran had encouraged her to face her fears. It was all she had to rely on at this point. Yes, whenever doubt started to creep in or obstacles seemed to be insurmountable, there was always one guaranteed cure: *A Day with Gran.*

"We have to get out of here," Alex and Marvin whispered.

"But how are we going to do that?" snapped Josie. "You two are the superheroes. What kind of power do you have up your sleeves to get us out of this mess?"

"Josie, not now," said Olivia.

"Yes, now. This entire situation is his fault," Josie said, pointing at Marvin. "Taking us down the wrong path; look at us locked up in a cage like rats."

"I guess that you have all of the answers,

right?" interjected Alex.

"Wait, you guys. We are in this together, and we have to work as a team to get out of this," Olivia reasoned.

Marvin sat for a moment with his head down and his hand in his pocket. Then, he looked up and pulled out a shiny object. It was a special coin called The Challenger. His grandfather had given it to him. When Marvin was confused and didn't know what to do, he would rub the coin and ask for guidance.

"What is that?" asked Josie.

"Umm, let me think, just give me a minute!" said Marvin as he listened to the creatures conversing with one another.

"You better think fast, or we're going to be human stew."

"That's it! I got it!" exclaimed Marvin.

"Isabella and Maria, sing something in Spanish."

"What do you want us to sing?"

"Anything…just do it, now!" he said with urgency.

And so, they started to sing, "*Mece mi bebé en la copa del árbol.* Rock a-my baby on the treetop…" As they sang, the creatures sat down and started to relax.

"Keep doing it. It's working, it's working!" he shouted, as the creatures started to drift off to sleep. He remembered that his grandfather had told him before they disappeared that if they were ever captured by the creatures to have someone sing a song. The song would put them to sleep.

"Now that they are asleep, how are we going to get out of this cage?" asked the twins.

"I know how! Ming-Lin, give me one of

your hair pins." Olivia reached her arm through the small opening between the bars on the cage. She tried picking the lock with the pin, but it wouldn't open.

"Gosh, I can't do it!"

"But you have to, you're our only hope. The creatures are asleep now, but we don't know for how long," said Alex.

"Just take a deep breath and concentrate," encouraged the twins.

One of the creatures started to move, but he didn't wake up.

Ming-Lin sat with her eyes closed and fingers crossed, and she seemed to be mumbling a mantra of some sort.

Determined, Olivia tried picking the lock again. She held her breath as she bit on her bottom lip, focusing only on the lock. One slight turn to the left, then to the right—she was trying desperately not to bend the pin. She repeated this method a few times. Then they heard a click inside of the lock. They all jumped with joy!

"Shhhh, we have to be very quiet," Alex reminded them.

They calmed down and snuck past the sleeping monsters, trying not to step on them or make a sound. Once they reached the opening of the lair, they ran for their lives. They reached the fork in the road once again.

Out of breath, Olivia asked, "What were those things?"

The twins replied, "Growlers! Remember the first night you all came to the tree house, and you told us that you heard a loud noise when you were up in the tree? Well, that noise was the Growlers. They come out when it's raining, and they like the sound of the thunder. It calls to them."

"You told us that it was okay to take the road to the left. First, you get us lost, then you almost get us eaten alive by those creatures," Josie shouted as she pointed her finger at Marvin.

"We are all upset and scared, but yelling at Marvin isn't going to help us right now. We have to work together and stay positive," Olivia pleaded.

"She's right, though. It's all my fault," confessed Marvin. "I didn't believe. My grandfather told me that I must always believe in myself. Deciding to take the path to the left was a rush in judgment. I didn't want to embarrass myself by not knowing which way to go. I put all of us at risk, and I'm not a good leader."

"Okay, okay, let's all just put our heads together. We have to find a way out of this. I think that we should go to the other path, to the right of the fork, or go back to the tree house," suggested Alex.

They decided to vote on it, and the majority agreed to go to the right of the fork in the road. They had come too far to turn back. They walked what seemed like just a few feet and saw that this path was much like the path near the tree house. There were flowers, birds, trees, and all sorts of animals. Maybe it was the Creek of Blossoms. It looked the same, but how could it be? Nothing was for certain anymore after what they'd been through. They had gotten all mixed up with their directions, so anything could be possible, really.

Olivia and Josie were now leading the

way. Alex and Marvin were walking slowly in the back. Marvin was sad and disappointed in himself for leading them directly to the Growlers.

Alex placed his hand on his shoulder, "Don't beat yourself up about it. We're all safe, and that's what matters."

Marvin nodded, but he still felt bad about what had happened and knew that he had to find the courage to believe again.

"There's a place where we can rest for a while," said Olivia as she pointed ahead.

They discussed what to do next. Should they rest or keep going? It was not storming on this side of the path, so they felt they would be safe from the Growlers, at least for now. Marvin lay on his back, looking up at the sky. He thought about his family most during tense times like this—how much he missed them and how happy they were before they disappeared. He often wondered if he would ever see them again.

But having Alex around made it bearable. He was his best friend. He was loyal and always had Marvin's back. No matter what happened, he could always count on him, especially when they were in a stressful situation—like the one currently staring them straight in the face.

8

The Basket

There was a small light in the tree above them. The light moved from one branch to the other, like it was dancing on the tree limbs. It was at first very high in the tree, and then it made its way down to the lower branches. It stayed there for a while and then disappeared.

They could hear birds singing and the sound of running water from the creek. This side of the path was breathtaking; there were rabbits, ducks, squirrels, butterflies, deer, and even a couple of foxes racing around. It was enchanting and peaceful. They saw a field of flowers over near the edge of the forest. In the middle of the grassy area was a blanket. It had a large wicker basket on it. They hadn't noticed it before, so they all raced over. Alex reached down and opened the basket, and it was filled with wonderful treats: sandwiches, fruit, and even cake! But how did it get there? Whose food was it? They looked around, but didn't see anyone. They were very hungry and wondered if they should just eat a little bit.

"Maybe we shouldn't eat any of it since it doesn't belong to us," said Olivia.

"We'll only eat what we need and leave a note for the owner," replied Marvin.

"There's enough food here for an army; they won't miss the small amount that we'll take," Josie chimed in impatiently.

They agreed to only eat what they needed to get over their hunger pangs.

The soothing sound of the birds singing and the running water of the creek in the distance helped them relax. The animals gathered around the children as they ate. The ducklings wobbled onto the blanket next to Olivia as she greeted them. "Hello, pretty ducklings!" They quacked, as if they were saying hello back to her. Then the deer and foxes approached.

"This is a wonderful place. It's almost magical," said Josie, as even she was calm now.

Surprisingly, she was no longer upset

about missing her baseball game or getting lost and captured earlier. She stretched out on the blanket with her hands folded behind her head and her ankles crossed. "Ah, this is nice. I could stay here forever!" she said as she closed her eyes and smirked.

They were all very happy—happier than they had ever been. A breeze was blowing, and the sun was shining, but it wasn't overly hot. As the wind blew, the flowers swayed. As they swayed, they could hear a voice—a mesmerizing voice at that.

It was whispering, "Believe in yourself, and all things are possible."

The phrase repeated several times, and then the voice faded away. As this was happening, the children drifted off to sleep, with their bellies full and their minds at peace.

9

The Chickapea

As they all sat up, stretching and yawning from their short nap, they felt energized and ready to take on the world. It was as if they had slept for hours, instead of only a few minutes. As they gathered their things, they could feel a sense of purpose in the air. They looked around in amazement at all of the beauty that this remarkable place displayed.

As they walked back toward the path, they saw a tiny light. At first, Marvin thought it was just the sun reflecting, but it wasn't. As they moved closer, it seemed to be moving away, until finally they caught up to it.

"It's as if it's alive," observed Olivia.

She reached out to touch it, and it tickled. She laughed and tried to touch it again. And once again, it tickled her fingers. They all tried. Then the glowing light started to change into a small figure. It was beginning to come to life right before their very eyes!

"Mirada, mirada!" exclaimed the twins.

They all looked and couldn't believe what they saw. There in front of them was a tiny girl, and not just a tiny girl, but a tiny girl that also

had wings—gorgeous, translucent wings.

"What is it? Where did she come from? Will she hurt us?" asked Ming-Lin, as she nervously stepped back.

"No, she won't hurt us," Marvin said with confidence.

Alex leaned in to get a closer look, "Hello. What is your name?"

They could see her moving her lips, but they couldn't hear anything. She flew over, reached into one of the flowers, and pulled out some pollen. The children ran behind her. She sprinkled the pollen once in the air. As she did this, the children were now able to hear her.

"Hello, my name is Pinkel. I'm a Chick-apea fairy."

Marvin beamed with excitement. "My grandfather told me stories about you. I mean, about the Chickapeas."

"So he wasn't telling the truth, huh?" said Olivia as she nudged Josie.

The twins and Ming-Lin were giggling in the background.

"You don't have to rub it in. Okay, I was wrong. I'm not too big to admit it. I'm sorry for doubting you, Marvin."

Marvin smiled and shook his head, accepting her apology.

Pinkel playfully flew in the direction of the blanket, and they ran behind her. "Did you enjoy the food?" she asked.

"Yes, did you leave it there for us?" questioned the twins.

She winked as she landed on the basket. The children sat down around her.

"What are you doing here?" asked Ming-

Lin.

"I'm the only Chickapea left in the forest. It's my duty to do something to make these storms go away."

"What will happen if you don't?" inquired Olivia.

"The storms will keep the magical flower from blooming again."

"Marvin told us the story about the Rainbow Flower," said Ming-Lin.

Pinkel smiled and continued, "I know that it's sunny on this side of the forest, but the other side is still dark. The flower will only bloom if both sides are sunny."

"How can we help? What do you need us to do?" asked Josie.

"Many years ago, the last big storm came that blocked the sun, and the Rainbow Amulet which contained magical pollen was stolen by the Growlers."

"You mean those horrible creatures in the cave?" asked Ming-Lin.

"Yes. The amulet is hidden somewhere in their lair. I've tried to get it, but when I get close to the lair, I become weak and unable to fly. If we can bring back the Rainbow Flower, the Growlers would sleep forever."

"We can help you," Marvin and Alex said with brave enthusiasm.

10

The Capture

Now, how were they going to get back into the lair? They contemplated for a while, and then it came to them. They would get the Growlers to capture them again! Isabella and Maria could sing their song. It would put them to sleep, and then they could get the amulet. It was an easy plan.

Or at least it seemed easy, in theory, Olivia thought to herself.

Pinkel followed along with them until they reached the fork in the road. "This is as far as I can go."

"We understand. We'll be back soon," said Olivia.

"I really appreciate all that you guys are doing to help me. The forest needs more protectors like you."

Josie smiled. Now, she finally understood what it meant to be a protector—to care about others and do whatever it took to keep them safe.

As Pinkel flew away, the children waved goodbye. They stood at the fork in the road for a few minutes.

"Okay, we are all ready for this, right?" asked Marvin.

"Yes!" shouted Maria and Isabella.

They went over the plan one more time, just to make sure everyone was on the same page, before they began walking down the path. As they started along their journey, it was quiet at first. Then—just as they had hoped—the rain and thunder started. Like clockwork, they could hear heavy breathing, loud footsteps, and growling noises coming up the path.

"Take your places," whispered Marvin.

Olivia and Ming-Lin ran over behind a tree, while the others hid behind the big rock. Although everything was going as planned, the kids were still frightened.

As the creatures approached, Olivia screamed to get their attention. When the creatures stopped to look, the other children ran out. What followed was complete chaos—kids running in all directions, Growlers racing behind them.

Marvin yelled to Alex, "I'm going to slow down so they'll be able to catch me."

Alex pretended to trip over a stone. As he fell to the ground, one of the Growlers scooped him up over his shoulder. Screaming like wild cats, Maria, Isabella, and Olivia ran behind a cluster of bushes and were snatched up within a matter of seconds.

Just as they had so craftily planned, they were captured. While in the cage, they began to look around in order to see if they saw the Rainbow Amulet. Unfortunately, they didn't see anything. The amulet had to be there somewhere.

11

The Power of Teamwork

The Growlers were starting to move around in the cave. Then they began to kneel. As Olivia and the others looked toward the opening of the lair, they saw a huge creature. It was bigger than all of the others. It had a red mark down the center of its face. Its horns were massive with extra small horns growing on them.

Marvin whispered, "It must be the leader."

It walked over to the cage, looked in at them, and started to speak. It said, *"Hola pequeños. Seran una golosina sabrosa."* The twins gasped.

"What's wrong?" asked Olivia.

The twins translated what he had said: "Hello, little ones. You will be a tasty treat."

As the leader walked away, he gestured for the other Growlers to rise and get the hot water ready. They could hear the Growlers getting louder and more aggressive.

"Okay, guys, it's time for phase two of the plan," declared Alex.

"Mece mi bebé en la copa del árbol," the twins sang.

"It's not working," replied Olivia.

"Keep singing. The leader is here, so his power is strong. We have to keep trying! Sing louder," encouraged Marvin as he surveyed the room.

"I think I see something," shouted Alex. "Look over there, near the fire. It's something shiny."

Marvin and Olivia looked, but it was only the reflection of a piece of silver.

One of the Growlers came over to the cage and unlocked it. He reached in and tried to grab Alex. Alex shouted, "Get away from me, you stinking monster!"

Marvin was holding onto Alex's shirt, pulling him back away from the Growler. "Stop! Leave my friend alone. Let go of him now!"

He reached in again, but this time, Alex kicked him square in the nose. The creature grimaced as he covered his nose in pain. As another creature rushed over to the cage, the sound of a loud whistle came out of nowhere.

"Mirada, mirada," shouted the twins. "It's Josie and Ming-Lin."

During all of the commotion, they hadn't noticed that they weren't even in the cage with them. When the others had gotten captured, the two of them had hidden themselves. While trying to decide what to do next, Josie remembered that she had her dad's referee whistle in her backpack. Her dad had given it to her and instructed her to blow the whistle if she was ever in danger. She knew that now was as good a time as any.

The Growlers covered their ears because the sound made them extremely dizzy. Ming-Lin bravely ran over to the cage to help the others out, while the creatures were distracted. Josie kept blowing the whistle with all of her might. She blew harder and harder, as her friends all raced to get out of the cave. But Olivia thought about the promise they had made to Pinkel to find the Rainbow Amulet.

She and Marvin looked at each other, and without saying a word, Olivia pulled out her watch and Marvin pulled out his coin.

"I'm not sure if we can find it. Maybe it's not here," said Marvin gloomily.

"It is here! We just have to believe it! Please don't give up now," encouraged Olivia.

Standing in the middle of the cave, they held hands, closed their eyes, and started thinking about the amulet. They could feel the power and magic of the amulet come into their minds, and then into their hearts. They started to believe they could find it. All of a sudden, a bright light appeared from beneath the throne of the leader.

Alex shouted, "It's the Rainbow Amulet! We found it!"

He ran over to pick it up, but a large, hairy hand also reached down. It was the leader, and he was trying to keep the amulet from them!

Once Isabella, Maria, and Ming-Lin saw what was happening, they rushed back over. They held hands with Marvin and Olivia, and then linked hands with Alex as he reached for the amulet with his free hand. As they all held hands, the twins began to sing. Marvin, Olivia, Ming-Lin, and Alex joined in, too.

They all sang in harmony: *"Mece mi bebé en la copa del árbol.* Rock a-my baby on the treetop..."

It was working! The leader was starting to get sleepy! It took their united effort of bravery, positivity, and confidence to make it work. As he drifted off to sleep, so did the other creatures.

Josie realized that it was all right for her to stop blowing her whistle. Alex grabbed the Rainbow Amulet, and they ran out of the lair! They ran until they reached the field of flowers where Pinkel was waiting for them.

They yelled out to her, "We got it! We have the Rainbow Amulet!"

Pinkel was ecstatic. "Now, we have to take it to the place where the Rainbow Flower once bloomed."

"Let's go!" shouted the twins.

When they reached the spot, Pinkel explained, "We have to sprinkle the magical pollen from the amulet on the ground before sunset, or it won't work. It needs the sunlight to grow."

As she sprinkled the pollen, she asked them to close their eyes and imagine with her that the flower was growing. She said, "You have to believe. Believe, and anything is possible."

They started to feel the ground tremble beneath them. Then, the wind started to blow, and the animals all gathered around. You could feel the goodness of all the happy hearts. Once they opened their eyes, they saw the Rainbow Flower starting to come up from out of the earth. The magical flower was back and blooming!

They all danced around, laughing and hugging each other. Now that the flower was back, the Growlers would sleep forever. All of the fairies could finally come back home!

Josie whispered to Marvin, "Does this mean your family will come back?"

Marvin smiled. "Anything is possible if you believe."

12

Let Class Begin

"Olivia! Olivia Kennedy!" It was Ms. Ellis calling her name. "Are you daydreaming again, young lady?" she asked.

"I'm sorry, Ms. Ellis. I guess my mind drifted off for a minute or two."

"I'm trying to call attendance so we can

get started with last night's assignment, but you are somewhere else it seems." She closed the attendance book. "Okay, everyone turn to page 25 in your math books. Miss Olivia, since you have a case of the daydreamer's fever today, please come to the board. You can do the first problem."

She was so excited about her adventure that she would gladly do all of the math problems.

Soon, the first half of class was over, and it was time for break. After getting her lunch out of her locker, she rushed to find her friends. On nice sunny days, Ms. Ellis would let them have lunch outside. She spotted the group across the yard. Olivia raced over to the picnic table. She was talking so fast they couldn't understand a word that she was saying.

"Wait, slow down!" pleaded Maria and Isabella as they put away their notepads. They loved to sing and write songs. They each had a small, pink notebook that they carried everywhere to jot down lyrics. They were very talented and could make up a song about anything.

Ming-Lin was unwrapping her sandwich as Alex and Marvin walked up.

"What's going on?" they asked.

Olivia took a deep breath and started telling them about her daydream. She reminded them about the flashing light she saw on the way to school this morning.

"You mean the distress signal?" joked Josie.

"Is that what it was?" asked the twins.

"Of course. If Olivia said it was a distress signal, then that's what it was," exclaimed

Ming-Lin.

"It could be anything—a piece of metal from a plane or a bird with silver feathers, and the sun was just reflecting off of it," explained Josie.

"Yes, or it could be a small spacecraft that crashed into the treetop, and the alien was wearing a shiny suit, and that's what she saw," said Marvin.

"Yep, we've read about these things in our comic books. There are all kinds of creatures out in the faraway galaxies. Tell us more, Olivia," said Alex.

Olivia eagerly continued with the story. By the time she got to the part about the Growlers, even Josie was captivated—which wasn't easy to accomplish. They heard Ms. Ellis calling out to them. Lunch break was over.

"Oh gosh, don't stop! The story was getting good," pleaded Josie, as she stomped her foot.

The twins giggled.

Knowing that she wouldn't have time to finish, Olivia invited them to her house after school.

13

After School

On the way home, they passed by the tree where Olivia had seen the bright light shining from that morning. The light wasn't flickering; she smiled as she thought about her daydream.

"How was your day?" asked Olivia's mom.

"It was great. Can I go play when we get home?" questioned Olivia.

"Only after you do your homework."

"Yes, ma'am."

When they arrived home, Olivia ran upstairs to her room, so she could quickly finish her homework. About an hour later, she hurried downstairs and announced, "I'm finished! Now can I go outside? I only want to go in the backyard."

"Yes, but be back in by six o'clock. Your father will be home from work, and dinner will be ready."

Olivia rushed out the backdoor. Her friends were waiting for her beneath the huge weeping willow tree. Josie was leaning with her back on the tree, looking at her baseball cards. Ming-Lin and the twins were sitting on the

ground with legs crossed, exchanging hair accessories and giggling as they made up songs about
the ribbons and pins. Marvin and Alex were exchanging issues of their latest comic books.
Olivia raced up, beaming with excitement, with
her goldflower watch in hand. They stopped
what they were doing and gathered around her.

"Can you start from the beginning?"
asked Josie.

"*Por favor, por favor.* Please, please," pleaded Maria and Isabella.

"Yes, I want to hear the part again about
the fairy. I love fairies. They wear the cutest
outfits!" gushed Ming-Lin.

"No, I want to hear how Marvin the Marvelous saved the forest from the Growlers and
rescued the damsel in distress," exclaimed
Marvin.

"What damsel in distress? She said a distress signal. You've been watching too many superhero movies!" joked Josie.

"Never mind all of that. Just let her tell us about the daydream, guys," said Alex.

Olivia was more than happy to repeat what she had told them earlier on the playground. Beaming with delight, she told them about the Rainbow Amulet, Pinkel, the Growlers, the cave, and the magical flower. She didn't leave out one single part; every detail was shared. She made hand gestures, growling sounds, cries of fear, and squeals of enthusiasm. She was all over the place, jumping and bouncing around as she acted out her story. She was tempted to get in the tree and pretend to be a fairy—like Pinkel—but then remembered she wasn't allowed to do that because she might fall and get hurt.

Her six friends meant the world to her, and they loved listening to her tales of adventure. It made them feel as though they were truly a part of her whimsical journey.

Because we all know that in Olivia's mind, there is always a thrilling quest waiting just around the corner. The only remaining question is: *What adventure could be next?*

Also by
Chiffon Strickland Jenkins

 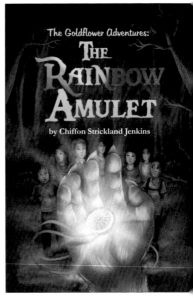

Now Available at:
Goldfloweradventures.com

53512384R00060

Made in the USA
Columbia, SC
16 March 2019